My Life in the Mountains

Eliza Robbins

Rosen Classroom Books and Materials
New York

My name is Charissa. I live in the Rocky Mountains in Colorado.

Deer live in the mountains, too.

I go to school at home.
My mom is my teacher.

There is a lot of snow in the mountains in the winter.

Flowers grow on the mountains in the spring.

I like to play outside in the clean mountain air.

Words to Know

deer

flowers

mountains

snow